The Fortress of the Treasure Queen

A Magical World Awaits You
Read

THE SECRETS OF DROON

The Fortress of the Treasure Queen

by Tony Abbott

Illustrated by David Merrell

Cover illustration by Tim Jessell

A
LITTLE APPLE
PAPERBACK

SCHOLASTIC INC.
New York Toronto London Auckland Sydney
Mexico City New Delhi Hong Kong Buenos Aires

For more information about the continuing saga of Droon,
please visit Tony Abbott's website at
www.tonyabbottbooks.com

ISBN 0-439-66157-9

12 11 10 9 8 7 6 5   5 6 7 8 9/0

Printed in the U.S.A.
First printing, October 2004

For Lucy and Jenna,
friends and treasures
who make each other sparkle

Contents

One

Mission of Mystery

Eric Hinkle wasn't alone as he hopped around his room, trying to pull on his left sock.

"That might be easier if you sat down," squeaked a high voice.

Eric flopped on his bed and stared.

On his dresser stood a small bird carved of black wood. Its wings were folded. It had two green dots for eyes.

It was talking to him.

"I still can't believe it," said Eric. "A magical bird is talking to me!"

"Droon has lots of magic," said the bird.

Eric knew that, of course.

Droon was a vast realm of magic, a land of wizards and sorcerers, of enchanted castles and floating cities, of serpent-filled seas and misty islands. Droon was the secret world Eric and his friends Julie and Neal had discovered one day under his basement stairs.

On their first adventure there, the three friends had met Keeah, an awesome princess just learning her wizard powers.

She had become their best Droon friend.

Since then, Eric and Julie had gained powers of their own. Julie could fly, and Eric could shoot silver sparks from his fingers, speak silently to his friends, and even cast weird ancient spells.

And Droon was where Eric had found the strange talking bird.

"If you're magical, do you know the future?" he asked it.

"I don't even know the past!" said the bird. "Someone must have put a memory spell on me. It's all a mystery. I think I'm on a mission, but I know only two things about it —"

"My name," said Eric. "You called to me."

"Yes. Your name," said the black bird.

It had happened in a place called the Isle of Mists. Eric remembered how stunned he had been when the bird had first spoken his name. Then he remembered how he had slid the bird into his pocket without telling anyone and how he had brought it home.

"And one other thing," said the bird. " 'The hands of the sorcerer.' I have no idea what that means!"

"It sounds to me like a warning," said Eric, sliding his feet into his sneakers. "'The hands of the sorcerer?' It probably means Sparr. Sparr is the worst sorcerer I know!"

That was true. Since just about forever, Keeah and her parents, King Zello and Queen Relna, along with their spider troll friend, Max, had been trying to keep Droon free from the clutches of the wicked and powerful Lord Sparr. Eric, Julie, and Neal had joined them many times to battle the sorcerer.

Then, on their latest adventure, while Sparr was using his Coiled Viper to wake the Emperor Ko from his ancient sleep, something unbelievable happened.

Ko, the four-armed, bull-headed ruler of beasts, did come alive and was now back in modern Droon. But Sparr himself got zapped back to when he was a child.

The sorcerer was now their age!

"Talk about mystery," said Eric. "Sparr is now in Jaffa City. With Keeah! He asked us to help him. But maybe it's a trick. Maybe your mission is to warn us — to warn *me* — against him."

"That would mean I'm on a dangerous mission!" said the bird.

Eric frowned. "We're all pretty much in danger now, since I broke the first rule of the stairs."

That was true, too. From the very beginning, the wizard Galen had told the kids not to bring anything from Droon into their world. If they did, things would start moving between the worlds.

Things.

Or people.

"That rule was broken once before," said Eric, shivering to remember it. "And my dad got zapped into Droon! I have to take you back before something like that happens again. And as soon as Neal and Julie get here, I will —"

A sudden burst of laughter came from outside. Running to his window, Eric saw Julie and Neal heading across his backyard.

"Finally!" he said, his heart thumping. "Come on, mystery bird!" He slipped the small figure carefully into his pocket and ran downstairs.

When he got to the kitchen, his mother was stirring something in a mixing bowl. His father was bending over, peering into the oven.

Eric stopped. He sniffed. "I smell —"

"Cookies!" said Neal, bursting in the back door and sticking out his hands. "Two, please!"

Julie closed the door behind him, laughing.

"Sorry, kids," said Mrs. Hinkle with a smile. "These cookies aren't for us."

"We want to welcome the new family up the street," said Mr. Hinkle. "They're moving in today —"

Neal grinned. "Then I'm just in time. You can't give new neighbors bad cookies. As the person with the most cookie experience, I have to test them."

Eric felt the bird flutter in his pocket. "Guys," he said, "I really need to show you something."

"And what I really need," said Mrs. Hinkle, "is the big cookie jar from the attic. Can you kids run upstairs and find it?"

"Upstairs?" said Eric. The bird was still fluttering.

"Our first mission of the day," said Julie. "I mean . . . wow! A mission? Great!"

"All right," said Eric with a low grumble. He quickly led his friends upstairs, past his room and up a second set of steps to the top of the house. The attic was filled with dusty cartons, old suitcases, exercise equipment, bags of clothes, and lots of baby toys.

"Kind of a mess," said Julie, looking around.

Eric drew in a breath. "Guys, we'll hunt for the jar in a minute. First, take a look at this —" He pulled the bird from his pocket. It sat in his hand for a second, then flew up to the rafters.

"Holy crow!" Neal gasped. "It looks like a toy. Where did you get that?"

"Eric!" said Julie, her eyes wide. "Don't tell me that bird is from Droon! You shouldn't have —"

"I know, I know. I broke the rules," said Eric. "But I couldn't help it. The bird spoke to me!"

"I did speak to him!" chirped the bird. "I'm on a mission. But I can't remember anything, except that I was sent to get Eric to help me."

"And something about 'the hands of the sorcerer,'" said Eric. "I'm pretty sure it's a warning about Sparr —"

"Uh-oh." Neal's eyes were fixed on a round brown jar next to a stack of suitcases. Written in big blue letters on it was the word COOKIES.

The jar was wobbling back and forth, ever so slightly. Then it began to spin faster and faster until, with a quiet *plink,* it vanished.

The three friends stared at the spot.

"Maybe I shouldn't have come?" said the bird.

Julie put her hand out to where the jar had been and waved it around. "It's gone. The spell has already started. Guys, we need to —"

"Right now!" said Neal.

"Oh, this is not a good thing!" said Eric.

"Don't forget me!" cried the bird. It flew down, Eric slipped it carefully into his pocket again, and they charged downstairs together.

When they got to the kitchen, Mr. Hinkle was stacking cookies on a plate. "Did you find the jar?"

"Uh, I think we'll look in the basement," said Julie.

"Yeah, maybe the jar is under some stuff down there," added Neal.

Yeah, Eric spoke silently to his friends. *Under the house. All the way — in Droon!*

They jumped down the basement steps and quickly pushed away some cartons stacked in front of a door under the stairs. Opening the door, they crowded into a small closet and turned on the light dangling from the ceiling.

Eric shut the door behind them.

"Guys," he said, "I know I broke a major rule. But maybe we can stop stuff from moving between the worlds before anything else goes. Just let me tell Keeah, all right?"

"Of course," said Julie.

"You bet," said Neal. He switched off the light.

An instant later — *whooosh!* — the floor vanished, and the kids found themselves on the top step of a staircase curving away from the house.

Twenty steps below drifted the gauzy pink clouds of the sky of Droon.

Together the three friends circled down the steps, slowly at first, then more quickly.

When they pushed through the clouds, they spied a patch of dark woods surrounded by fields. Far in the distance rose the bright towers and gleaming walls of Jaffa City. The afternoon sun shone orange on the palace's great dome.

"It's always amazingly beautiful here," said Julie. "Keeah is so lucky."

"I hope *we're* lucky," murmured Eric.

Suddenly — *shoooom!* — a bright green carpet darted down through the clouds and flew toward them.

On it sat Keeah herself, clutching the carpet's front edge. Next to her was their spider troll friend, Max.

Julie waved. "Keeah, Max —"

"Hurry!" said Keeah, slowing the carpet next to the stairs. "It's Sparr. He's gone!"

"Gone?" Eric shot a look at his friends. "Oh, no!"

Without another word, the kids leaped from the stairs to the carpet, and it lifted up and away over the shadowy woods.

Two

Enemies New and Old

Whoo-shooom! The carpet dipped between the trees, circled a broad clearing, then climbed up again.

"We have a missing sorcerer on our hands!" chirped Max. "Actually, he's not on our hands. In fact, he's not anywhere!"

Eric swallowed hard as they skimmed the high trees. "Keeah, maybe it's my fault that Sparr vanished. Look —"

When he pulled the little bird from his

pocket, Keeah nearly fell off the carpet. "Eric —"

"I had to take it," he protested. "It spoke to me!"

"I really did!" said the bird. "I'm on a mysterious mission. So mysterious, not even *I* know what it is!"

As they swooped over a field rolling down to the coast, Eric told how he had taken the bird from Droon and what it had said to him.

"It involves me," he said. "Sparr, too, I think."

"But the spell has already started," said Julie. "Mrs. Hinkle's cookie jar got zapped here."

"A cookie jar?" asked Max.

Neal nodded. "I know what you're thinking, but no, it didn't have any cookies in it."

Aiming the carpet at a distant beach,

Keeah sighed. "Okay. We have to find the jar and get it back to your mom. But I don't think Sparr is in the Upper World. This morning we found him studying maps in Galen's tower. The next thing we knew, he was gone —"

"Until now!" gasped Neal. "There he is. He's still in Droon!"

Neal pointed at the white beach ahead. There, huddled behind a row of jagged rocks, was a small boy in a long black cloak.

The bird's green eyes glowed. "Sparr? The sorcerer? We're flying to him?"

Eric gulped. "Right. The warning. I'd better hide you!"

As he hid the bird again, Keeah banked the carpet into a slow circle over the beach. Woven of rich green threads, the carpet was decorated with stars and triangles. From each corner dangled a silky purple spiral.

"I remember this cool carpet," said Neal. "Some dude named Pasha made it. Way back on our first adventure, we used it to escape the creepy city of Plud."

"We used it to escape, all right," said Eric. "From Sparr, remember —"

Keeah swung the carpet carefully down behind a grassy dune some distance from Sparr. Together, the five friends got off and peered over the crest of the dune.

The moment they did — *pooomf!* — a sudden blast of sand sprayed up at them, tumbling them back down the dune. Before they could get to their feet, Sparr leaped like a blur across the sand toward them.

"What are you doing here?" he hissed. "I almost zapped you!"

"You left the palace!" snapped Max.

"I had to," he said. "And there's the reason — take a look!"

As he said this, the clouds suddenly

tore open above them, and two large creatures flapped down toward the beach.

"Holy cow!" gasped Julie, crouching behind the dune. "Flying beasties!"

"Pretty ugly ones!" said Neal.

"Exactly," whispered Sparr. "Now watch —"

While everyone else peeked over the dune, Eric studied Sparr out of the corner of his eye. The boy was young, like them, with a normal enough face, except that behind each ear grew the little nub of what looked like a fish fin. Even if Sparr was young, Eric thought, those fins marked him as a sorcerer.

Thwapp! Thwapp! The two dark creatures approached, and the kids saw that they were covered with ragged gray scales. Curled spikes stuck out of their heads in every direction. Their eyes were darting, small, and red.

Scanning the beach but seeing no one, the beasts thudded to the ground. The larger of them clawed the sand while the other made squealing and hissing noises.

"They're plotting something," said Sparr.

Eric shared a look with Keeah.

Plotting? he said to her silently. *I wonder if Sparr is plotting right now. Against us —*

Shhhh! Keeah grabbed Eric by the arm.

At once, he realized that Sparr might understand their magical silent talk. After all, Sparr was the son of a great wizard and the brother of Galen.

But the boy's expression didn't change. Looking over the rock as if he heard nothing, he said, "The beasts are finished. They'll circle, then go."

Sure enough, flapping their heavy wings, the two beasts lifted up, circled the beach once, then set off across the sea.

"What are they up to?" asked Julie.

When it was safe, Sparr climbed the dune and gazed at the beasts. "Ko has lots of plans and servants on lots of missions all across Droon. If one plan messes up, another might not. But every plan has the same purpose —"

"To take over Droon," grumbled Max.

Sparr nodded.

"You know those creepy guys pretty well," said Eric, watching the two beasts fly farther and farther away.

Sparr's fins turned redder as he spoke. "I grew up with them."

From his cloak, he removed a rolled-up map.

"Princess, he did steal a map!" said Max.

"I was going to give it back!" protested Sparr, glancing from the map to the sea. "I don't know how, but since this morning I knew beasts were coming. I had to find out where they were going and why. What's out there across the water? Is it Mikos, by any chance?"

Keeah looked over the waves, then traced her finger across Galen's old map. "Yes. The island of Mikos. The fortress of Queen Bazra."

"She steals treasure and collects magic there," said Julie.

Sparr began to smile. "I should have known. Bazra may have lots of magic in her treasure fortress, but those beasts are after only one thing."

The children stared at the boy.

"Are you going to make us ask?" said Eric.

Sparr took a breath. "Long ago, Ko built something. *Lightning Blade,* he called it. Or *King Stinger*. But mostly he called it the *Sword of Jaffa*."

Max shuddered. "I don't like that name."

"What is it, like, a big sword?" asked Neal.

Sparr shook his head. "I saw it once. It's a ship that moves under the water."

"A submarine?" asked Eric.

"Ko's big war machine," said Sparr. "His plan was — and is again, I guess — to attack Jaffa City. From below."

Keeah looked down the beach at the faraway port of the royal city, then back over the water. "We would never let him —"

"You don't know Ko like I do," said Sparr. "He wants . . . everything."

"Then why did you bring him back?" asked Eric.

Sparr turned to him. "I . . . I don't know. The grown-up me did it. All I know is that maybe all of us . . . together . . . can stop him. Don't you think we should try?"

He raised his sparking hands. "I mean, I could help —"

Eric remembered the bird's strange words.

The hands of the sorcerer.

"Uh, I'm not so sure," said Eric. "Maybe we should vote or something. Guys, team huddle. All of us except you, Sparr."

Grumbling, Sparr paced away behind the dunes.

"Can we trust him?" Eric whispered. "I know he's a kid. Like us, even. But he's Sparr. Does everybody remember when the Moon Scroll led us to Ko's palace? We saw young Sparr there. He wasn't so nice. And he already took Galen's map. And the bird gave me that warning, too —"

"Right," said Julie. "But Eric, you took the bird. . . ."

Eric sighed. "Okay. I took the bird. That was wrong. But 'the hands of the sorcerer' sure seems like a warning about Sparr. He really worries me —"

"But he looks younger this time," said Neal, glancing at Sparr. "His fins are smaller."

"And he says he's afraid of Ko," added Max. "I know I am."

Keeah watched Sparr staring out to sea, then kicking the sand. "I don't know. But I remember something Galen always told us. He said that nothing is evil to begin with."

"Right," said Julie. "And Sparr's mother was Queen Zara, don't forget. He's Galen's brother."

Eric glanced at Sparr. He looked so small, staring across the sea toward the island of Mikos. Watching, Eric found that he wasn't sure about the boy. Maybe Sparr really *was* afraid of Ko. Maybe he did want to stop the beast's plans. Maybe . . .

Finally, Eric nodded. "All right. Maybe we do need him. But if what my bird said really is a warning, we need to be careful. Uh, Sparr —"

The boy turned eagerly. "Yes?"

"You can come," said Keeah.

Sparr jumped. "Really? Thank you! This is great! We'd better hop on that carpet and get to Bazra's island as soon as we can. Come on, there's no time to waste!"

Watching Sparr race across the beach, with Julie, Neal, and Max chasing after him, Eric turned to Keeah. "I always knew we'd see Bazra's treasure fortress again," he whispered. "But I never thought Sparr would be on our side!"

Keeah smiled. "You can say that again. Come on."

Three

Dragon Eyes

It was already late afternoon when Keeah flew the green carpet away from the beach and up over the darkening waves. She flew at a breakneck speed until they could see the beasts just ahead of them, then slowed and steered a course that kept them just out of sight.

Julie and Neal huddled under a cloak. Max was in between them, his nose stuck in Galen's map.

"This is amazing," murmured Sparr, leaning into the rushing wind. "I feel so free! Since forever, I've been hidden away in one of Ko's palaces or another."

"In the Dark Lands?" asked Keeah.

The boy nodded. "When Ko went on his missions, he always left me behind, guarded by a beast called a moon dragon."

"Doesn't sound like fun," said Julie.

"Not fun," agreed Sparr.

"What else do you remember?" asked Neal.

As the carpet soared over the waves, the boy closed his eyes for a second, then opened them again. "The thing I most re-member is an attack on the Dark Lands. It was huge. Ko was wounded, and the dragon ship flew him away. I never saw him again —"

"You will," said Eric. "You brought him back."

Sparr glanced at Eric. "That's all pretty confusing. I find I have memories of me *older*. I'm grown-up and doing bad things. Like bringing Ko back to life. But that's so weird, isn't it?"

Max stared at Keeah, then lowered his head.

Sparr turned, the cold wind running through his hair. "Tell me . . . about me."

As Keeah drove the carpet faster toward the setting sun, the five friends told Sparr what they knew. That as an infant, he was kidnapped from the Upper World with his wizard mother, Queen Zara. That Zara died, and Ko brought him up. That he became a sorcerer of great power and the leader of the red warriors called Ninns. Even that the wizards Galen and Urik were his brothers.

"Zara," said Sparr, wincing as he spoke her name. "I remember her."

Upon hearing the queen's name, Eric found that his heart beat faster. It always did, though he had never understood why.

"My master Galen searched for you for years," said Max. "From the moment he made the rainbow stairs, he did nothing but look for you."

"But I was already lost!" cried Sparr.

Keeah put her hand on his cloaked shoulder. "Maybe you're found again —"

"Those icky beasts found something," said Julie. "Take a look!"

The two creatures they were following slowed, and out of the southern sky came a larger, darker shape. Four broad wings, ragged and spiked, waved up and down as if in slow motion. It approached the two beasts.

Sparr began to tremble. "Oh, please, no! Quick, fly us into a cloud! Hurry!"

Keeah jerked the carpet up into a passing wisp of pink and hovered there.

"Yikes, what is that thing?" said Neal.

Peering through the cloud, they watched the new beast approach. It was not huge, but its two pairs of wings were very long and covered by scales the color of night. It had toothy jaws, a thick tail, and powerful forelegs ending in long, black-nailed claws.

"It's a dragon." Julie shuddered. "An ugly one!"

It made a sudden piercing screech, and the two beasts slowed their flight even more.

"A moon dragon," murmured Sparr. He narrowed his eyes at the approaching beast. "He's the one Ko always left to guard me. He's much smarter than the others. His name is Gethwing."

"Gethwing?" grumbled Max. "I don't like that name, either."

"Nice," said Neal. "An ugly dragon who's smart. Can he please be just passing through?"

Gethwing joined the two other beasts and hovered in the air with them. Then he turned his large head down and pointed a claw at a small dot of land in the ocean far below.

"Let me guess," said Sparr. "The island of Mikos?"

Max scanned the map. "Of course!"

Together, the three beasts dipped slowly toward the island.

"If Gethwing's going to Mikos, then Ko sent him," said Sparr. "We have to be very careful. And very quick. Let's fly like the wind!"

Keeah smiled. "There's a reason this is my favorite Pasha carpet. It flies *faster* than the wind. Now — go!"

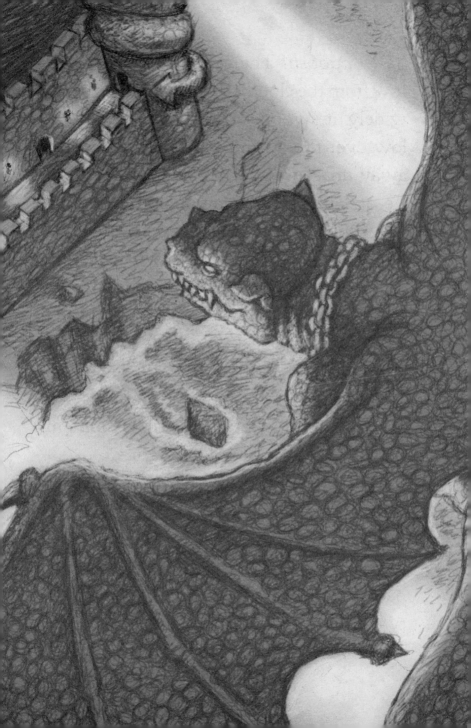

Fwoooosh! The carpet shot like an arrow from the cloud. Circling the three beasts widely, it swooped and dived like a swallow over the swampy shore, then dipped away unseen to the far side of the island. Keeah landed the carpet on one of the high gray cliffs before the beasts were even halfway there. They still flew toward the island very slowly, as if taking their time.

"We certainly beat the beasts!" chirped Max, squinting back across the sky.

Sparr looked out over the sea, too. "Gethwing's probably figuring out his plan of attack. He'll wait for the right moment. For now, let's find Ko's submarine."

"Yeah, but who says the *Sword of Jaffa* is even here?" asked Neal.

Sparr jumped up on a rock and scanned the island. Then he pointed to where the base of the fortress met the swamp. Between two large jagged rocks, the sea had carved a narrow inlet under the walls. The mouth of it was blocked by a thick iron gate whose bars were as curved and as sharp as fangs.

"Once," he said, "not long after Ko left on his dragon ship, but before he charmed himself and the other beasts to sleep, I heard that Bazra's treasure hunters had found his submarine. I'll bet it's been locked under the fortress since then."

"A fortress of magic," said Julie, turning to Eric. "Maybe we'll find your mom's cookie jar here, too."

"You think so?" said Eric. "That would be awesome!"

Sparr turned. "Something from the Upper World? Bazra would want it. And maybe not only Bazra. It would hold a lot of power in Droon."

"It holds a lot of cookies, too," said Neal. "But how will we ever get in?"

Between where they stood on the cliffs and the thick walls of the fortress first lay a field of high grass, then a wide stretch of bare ground that ended in a rocky chasm. The only way over it was a stone bridge that led right to the main fortress gate.

"That chasm is new," whispered Eric. "But I remember those guys."

Marching atop the fortress walls were dozens of spear-toting guards. Each one had two mean-looking, dog-shaped heads.

"There are more guards than before," said Max. "To protect against robbers."

"Robbers like us," said Keeah. She tugged one of the carpet's tassels and — *slurp!* — it shrank to the size of a handkerchief, which she slipped into a small pocket on her tunic. "Pasha was always very clever about storage," she said. "Now, let's go."

The small band wormed its way down a narrow pass through the cliffs, then paused at the base. At each corner of the fortress stood a tall tower shaped like a snarling dragon. Now, as night fell, searchlights blazed from the head of each dragon, their beams crisscrossing the island.

"The eyes of the dragons see all," said Max. "I hope they don't see us!"

Keeah stepped away from the cliffs. "Let's sneak quietly through the grass, then run carefully to the bridge."

"The key word being *sneak*," whispered Eric, eyeing the bright beams.

One searchlight streaked across the cliffs behind them.

"Also *quietly*," added Sparr, moving with Keeah into the high grass.

Another searchlight swept across the bridge.

"*Carefully* is a good thing, too —" said Julie.

A third beam flashed down from the fortress.

"Ooof!" said Neal. He stepped into a hole, lost his footing, and fell out of the grass onto the bare ground. He froze. "Maybe if I don't move, they won't see me —"

All three lights flashed right to him, the fortress gate shot open with a crash, the ground thundered, and a troop of dog-headed guards rushed out, barking and growling.

"I think they see you!" cried Eric. "Runnnnn!"

Four

Little Sparr, Big Ninn

"Back to the cliffs!" cried Keeah, dashing through the grass toward the rocks.

"Grooo-yaaa!" growled the two deep voices of the chief guard.

A moment later — *cling! plonk-k-k!* — a dozen three-edged spears whizzed across the grass, clanking finally against the distant cliffs.

"Sheesh!" whispered Neal, scrambling

to join his friends. "Why don't they just leave us alone so we can steal the sub?"

The guards waded quickly into the grass.

"They'll get us!" said Julie. "And throw us in a dungeon, and —"

"No they won't!" said Sparr. Looking both ways, he made a motion like throwing a ball, but nothing visible came from his hand.

A few moments later — *crack! crish! thump!* — the sound of footsteps went scurrying away through the grass.

The guards spun around instantly. The searchlights moved toward the sound.

"Everyone to the bridge —" hissed Sparr. "Really fast!"

While the guards charged to where Sparr had aimed his throw and the lights followed them, the kids raced across the dark ground to the bridge and huddled on a narrow ledge beneath it. They held their breath.

Finally, the chief guard growled from both heads. *"Ooog-rrrr!"*

His fellow guards took one last look around, then assembled again. On the chief's command, they marched toward the cliffs, picked up their spears, and headed away through the pass.

"Whew, that was close!" said Neal. "Good one, Sparr."

"Yeah," said Eric softly. "Thanks!"

Grinning, Sparr blew gently on his sparking fingers. "You're welcome."

Keeah held up her hand. "Wait a second. Why did the guards go through the pass? Did they go all the way down to the beach? Listen —"

They heard the sound of waves below, crashing first on the rocks then splashing against something hollow.

Max lifted his head. "A ship?" he whispered. "Is someone coming?"

A moment later, they heard the creaking of ropes and the clacking of oars. Soon the fortress searchlights were all trained on something moving in the black water below.

"Somebody's coming, all right," said Sparr. "Eric, boost me up!"

Startled, Eric put his hands together, and Sparr hoisted himself up. He crept to the top of the bridge, then craned his neck to look out past the swampy shore. His eyes widened. "Oh, my gosh!"

"What is it?" asked Neal.

"Let me see," said Keeah.

Eric boosted them and Julie up, too. Then he and Max scrambled up to the bridge by themselves. Eric's mouth dropped open when he looked. "Whoa —"

In the blaze of the searchlights, they saw a wooden sailing ship moored just beyond the swamp. A band of plump red creatures stomped down its crooked plank to the shore.

"Ninns!" said Keeah.

"Ninns?" gasped Sparr. "But don't they usually wear . . . armor?"

The Ninns were not covered in their usual black armor. They weren't waving swords around. They weren't storming off their ship for battle. The big red warriors were dressed in long, flowing robes, wildly colored scarves, and crowns of jewels and feathers.

Julie blinked. "Well, this is a new look for the Ninns. Pretty stylish!"

"Get down. Here they come!" said Eric.

The kids dived back under the bridge as the guards led the Ninns up over the cliffs and through the grass in single file. Two of the Ninns carried a golden chest between them.

"Ninns clean up pretty well," whispered Neal as the warriors marched overhead.

Eric nodded. "I bet they're working for Ko, just like Gethwing is —"

Sparr rubbed his forehead. "I don't think so. Seeing the Ninns makes me remember that . . . I sent them. This might have been my last order before I became small."

"You sent them here?" said Neal. "Terrific. Dragons and dog-faced guards aren't enough?"

The searchlights lit up the path to the main gate.

"But why?" whispered Keeah. "Why did you send them . . . like *that*?"

The boy's fins suddenly turned red. "Stay here!" With a swish of his cloak, Sparr leaped back up onto the bridge behind the last of the Ninns. He crept up to the warrior and tapped him on the shoulder.

The Ninn turned around while his companions kept going. A towering warrior, he lowered his feather-crowned head and gazed at Sparr with a large, dull face. Suddenly, the Ninn's eyes bulged. His mouth fell open. He began to quiver all over.

"My leader!" he said. "You are back again!"

As little Sparr waved his hand and the Ninn's round red face smiled, the kids listened but heard nothing. Sparr's fins glowed through every color of the rainbow, then turned a dull purple. The warrior pointed to the golden chest two of his fellow Ninns were carrying.

Finally, Sparr waved his hand again. "Yes, I see. Well, be on your way!"

The Ninn hiccuped loudly, spun on his heel, and joined the others now entering the fortress.

Just before the gate thudded shut and the searchlights swept the ground once more, Sparr dropped back down below the bridge. "Sorry, but I keep remembering things about myself. It seems I can read Ninn minds. That can be useful!"

"What did you find out?" asked Keeah. "Do you know why you sent them?"

"Bazra can't resist magic," said Sparr. "By pretending to be fancy magic traders, the Ninns got invited to the fortress. But once they're inside, they'll try to steal the *Sword of Jaffa*."

Neal chuckled. "The Ninns raided the costume shop to get past the guards!"

Sparr grinned. "Clever plan of mine, isn't it? I mean, wasn't it?"

"Uh-oh," said Julie. "It looks like Gethwing's got a plan now, too."

With a nearly silent flap of his four great wings, the moon dragon swooped finally to the island. Joined by the other beasts, he dropped below the distant cliffs.

Sparr's face grew serious. "We need to get in there —"

"But since I fell before, the fortress is probably on extra-high alert," said Neal.

Max watched the searchlights streaming across the ground in every direction. "We'll never get in now," he said.

"Right," said Sparr, "unless . . ."

Everyone turned to him.

Eric sighed. "Are you going to make us ask again?"

The boy grinned. "Unless . . . we don't sneak past the guards, or climb over the walls, or swim under the fortress, but march straight through the gate. Bazra will never refuse more magic traders. Who feels like dressing up?"

✳ Five ✳

Traders or Raiders?

Flick! Sloop! Swoo-ooosh! The air twinkled and sparkled under the stone bridge.

Max spun a wild array of spider-silk scarves and robes, then wrapped himself in a large orange turban. For herself, Keeah whipped up a glittering silver robe crossed with white and blue sashes.

Sparr twirled his hands and was instantly wearing a long white cloak. Fashioning a tall cone-shaped hat to match, he laughed. "White is the color of the good guys, isn't it?"

Eric stood there in green boots, green pants, a green vest, and a green cape that trailed behind him. Looking at Sparr, he found he was still unsure about him. Sparr seemed to be helping them, but Eric couldn't forget what the bird had said.

Were its words a warning? Is Sparr on our side or not?

Seeing Eric, Neal laughed. "Hey, Green Boy, call me Mr. Blue!" He wore a layered navy blue robe and a wide hat dangling with marsh flowers.

Julie's outfit matched Neal's, except that hers was pale yellow. "Princess Julie, at your service! What will we bring for magic? Bazra will want something special —"

"We'll think of something," said Sparr.

"With Gethwing on the island, things are getting more dangerous by the minute. Let's get inside and find Ko's sub."

As everyone scrambled to the top of the bridge, Eric paused. Ko's submarine wasn't the only thing they needed to find. Until the cookie jar was back in his own house again, both his world and Droon were also getting more dangerous.

Assembling in single file at the top of the bridge, the kids marched straight to the palace gate. Neal struck its big door three times. Trumpets sounded.

The chief of the guards stared down from the wall. "Who goes there?" he growled.

Deepening her voice as best she could, Keeah said, "Magic traders from . . . from . . ."

"Doobesh!" whispered Sparr. "They have good magic there. I think."

"From Doobesh!" said Keeah.

A minute or two of silence was followed by — *errrrch!* — and the heavy iron gate lifted. Inside was a long stone hall lined completely with armed dog-faced guards.

"This way!" barked the chief. He spun on his heel and marched in. The gate slammed shut behind them, and the friends followed the guard deeper into the fortress.

Eric looked into each new room they passed, hoping to catch a glimpse of the jar.

Marching next to him, Sparr gasped over and over. "Amazing . . . amazing!"

"That was where the Sapphire Star was on display," whispered Keeah, pointing to a treasure room with a high ceiling. "Before we stole it."

"And saved me with it!" whispered Max. Eric realized that the Star had saved Max, all right. From Sparr himself! He also noticed that the boy was trailing farther and farther behind the group. "Stay with us —"

Sparr shook his head. "The minute you said Sapphire Star, I remembered that I've met Bazra before. Well, the older me has. If she recognizes me, it'll blow our whole plan. I'm better off hunting around on my own, anyway. But good luck with Bazra!"

"Good luck?" whispered Eric. "You can't leave us here! Sparr!"

But the boy slipped down a side hallway. As he did, his white cloak faded away, and his familiar black cape reappeared around him. An instant later, he was gone.

The black bird began to flutter in Eric's pocket.

Right, thought Eric. *I don't trust him. I'm sorry, but I don't!*

"Follow!" snarled the guard. He turned a last corner then stopped before a large door. Opening it, he led the children into a vast room.

The room was blazing with light. Green and red banners hung from the walls. Garlands of ivy were draped from the ceiling and lit with miniature candles. The Ninns they had seen outside were clustered on one side of the room, straightening their costumes. On the other was a long table set with mounds of every kind of food and drink. In the center stood an empty throne made of black marble and topped with long, pointed antlers.

Behind the throne was a huge window that looked out on a large, lighted, inner courtyard of the fortress.

"This place is awesome!" whispered Julie.

"No kidding!" agreed Neal, his eyes scanning the table. "I hope we get to eat."

All of a sudden, the dog guards bowed toward a door at the far end of the room.

"Be careful, people," Eric whispered. "Bazra could be . . . be . . . *huh*?"

Bazra wasn't what he had expected.

She was short and round and wore a dazzling pink crown, a furry pink robe, and pink shoes. Even her cheeks were pink. They bulged as if they were filled with nuts.

"What a day! What a day!" Bazra chirped in a high voice as she pranced into the room. "Magic traders and more magic traders! Come forward, everyone! Show me what you have!"

The Ninns pushed rudely past the kids. On the count of three, they placed their hands over their chests, pointed their feet out, and began to sing.

We hope you like our fancy dress,
Because we bring to your fortress
The greatest magic ever seen —
It's all for you, Droon's treasure queen!

As the Ninns finished their song and everyone bowed, Julie and Keeah nudged Eric from both sides. Following their eyes, he looked through the giant window behind the throne. He stiffened as he saw a small, dark figure tiptoe across the courtyard.

Sparr! said Keeah silently.

As they watched, Sparr paused and looked up. Not more than a second later, a four-winged dragon swooped silently down from the sky and landed next to him. They seemed to be talking to each other

Sparr . . . and Gethwing! added Eric, unable to take his eyes away.

Bazra saw the children staring past her

and turned her head quickly toward the window. "What is going on —"

Suddenly, the bird in Eric's pocket quivered and tried to make its way out.

Quickly pulling it out, Eric yelled, "Queen Bazra! Look here! Magic!"

The queen jerked her head back. "Magic? Magic! I *do* love magic!"

As Gethwing flew up and Sparr scampered away across the courtyard, the little black bird flew around the room, spelling the name BAZRA in twinkling letters across the air.

"I love it!" cried Bazra. "Oh, show me more!"

"I can talk, O great Queen Bazra!" said the bird.

The queen's face lit up. "Excellent, excellent!"

"But we have better!" shouted one Ninn, glaring at the children. "Look!"

The two warriors carrying the golden chest stepped forward. With a flourish, they removed a single object and held it high for the queen to see.

The Ninns were holding an old brown jar with big blue letters painted on the side.

COOKIES

"We found it just this morning!" said the Ninn. "We knew you would like it!"

Eric couldn't breathe. He felt his heart leap. "My jar! It *is* here! It's *mine*!"

At once, Bazra stood, her eyes widening at the children. "I know magic things! That jar is from the Upper World! Which means *you* are from the Upper World! Upper Worlders in my fortress! Upper Worlders in my treasure collection!"

"Us? In her collection?" whispered Neal. "How's that going to work —"

Suddenly, Bazra began to change.

Her round pink cheeks shriveled as if she had sucked in all her breath. Her skin turned the color of ash. Her eyes, large and bright just a second before, now dwindled to shifty black dots in a sea of red. She became as gray as a ghost.

Julie made a face. "I think I liked her better before!"

The queen jerked up her hand. In it was a twisted wand, glowing with jagged black sparks. She waved it at the children.

Keeah backed up. "Uh . . . what does that do exactly?"

Bazra gave them all a cold grin. "Exactly? It freezes things. And people. Like you! Guards! Take the jar, take the bird, take it all! And block those doors. I'm gonna freeze me some magic traders!"

Six

Memories of the Future

"Grrrr-rooo!" growled the guards.

"But our song!" protested the Ninns. "We thought you liked it!"

"I'll like *you* in my collection!" cried Bazra. A beam of black sparks crackled from the wand. It missed the Ninns by inches but covered the floor with thick black ice.

"That's our cue to leave!" yelled Keeah.

She pulled Max to her, then flipped the green cloth from her robe and the flying carpet hovered before them.

"Come on, Eric, get on!" said Julie, running and sliding for the carpet.

"But my bird!" Eric shouted.

"I'll find you later!" chirped the bird. "I'm magical, remember!" It looped straight out of the hall, chased by several guards with a big net.

Watching until the bird was safely away, Eric scrambled onto the carpet. At the same time, he sent a bolt of silver light at the door. *Blam!* It scattered the queen's guards.

Instantly, the Ninns slid across the ice and out of the room, holding the jar high.

"We're right behind you!" said Keeah. "Carpet — go!"

"And I'm right behind *you*!" yelled Bazra. She jumped back to her antler throne. With a roaring sound, the throne lifted off the ground and shot into the hallway after them.

"Take your time!" Eric shouted back at her. He shot a blast at the queen. *Kkkkk!* In a bright burst of silver sparks, the queen tumbled off her throne and slid back into the room across the icy floor.

She toppled some guards, then struck the far wall with her head. *Thud!*

"See ya later, Bazra!" shouted Neal. "Or maybe never!"

Keeah shot the carpet down the hall outside the throne room.

"Princess, go left!" said Max.

"I'm going!" cried Keeah. She steered the carpet left into a stairway curving down from the main floor. Right away, they entered a series of twisting narrow passages. Keeah banked the carpet out of one corner and into another.

"They're trapped in the maze!" echoed one of the guards following them.

"Trapped?" said Julie. "I don't like the sound of that."

"Maze?" said Neal. "I don't like the sound of *that*!"

"Keeah, watch out!" said Eric. "A wall. A wall! *A wall!*"

Keeah jerked the carpet up, stopping inches from a stone wall. "Guys, there's only one chance to escape the guards. The old-fashioned way. Run!"

The kids tumbled off the carpet, tore off their costumes, and darted ahead into the winding tunnels. Eric ran as fast as he could, listening to the guards behind him and trying to follow the sound of Neal and Julie hustling ahead of him. Through one tunnel after another, he followed their steps until, slowing to catch his breath, he realized it wasn't his friends but the echo of his own footsteps that he had heard. He stopped.

"Julie?" he whispered.

No answer.

"Neal? Keeah? Max? Anyone?"

No answer.

Eric's heart pounded in his chest. *Oh, great!* he thought. *No bird. No cookie jar. No submarine. Sparr talking to Gethwing. And, oh, yeah, I'm lost in the maze of the treasure palace of a nutty, freezing queen! Could it get any worse —*

The passage behind him suddenly thundered with stomping feet.

Guards! He gasped. *I guess so!* Suddenly, two hands grabbed him and pulled him into a shallow alcove in the tunnel wall. "Hey —"

"Shhh!" hissed a voice.

The Ninns hustled by, still holding the jar high. They were chased by a dozen growling dog-headed guards. After they passed, a red spark flickered in the alcove, and Eric saw the outlines of a boy with fins.

"Sparr!" he whispered. "Did you know my jar was here? We saw you getting all chatty with Gethwing! Are you planning to give it to him —"

"No!" Sparr hissed. He looked at Eric in the light of the spark, then peered into the passage. "I knew the Ninns found the jar. When Gethwing saw me, I was terrified, but I tried to find out if he knew about the jar. He wanted to take me back to Ko! He tried to turn me to his side. I said no and had to make a run for it. You have to trust me."

Eric watched as Sparr shone his red sparks into the empty passage.

Trust you?

It was true that Sparr had told them about the sub and helped them get into the fortress. And just now, he had pulled Eric to safety when the guards were near.

Maybe. But what about the bird's warning?

"Come on!" whispered Sparr. Using his sparking fingers to guide the way, he was down the passage in an instant. He trotted up another tunnel, then stopped. "Oh!"

Eric moved up next to Sparr.

Before them was a treasure room. At the far end was an opening to another passage. In between stood rows and rows of twisted spears and staffs with gnarled tips. There were piles of dented helmets and shields. A mound of broken wands stood waist high. Against one wall was a great heap of yellow metal that Eric recognized as the remains of Sparr's car.

In the middle of all of it stood the tall black statue of a man with a spiked helmet and large jagged fins sticking up behind his ears.

Even as the distant echoes of guards came and went, Sparr gasped softly. "That's . . . me. . . . That's what I become!"

Stooping, he picked up a scroll that lay on the floor as if the black statue had dropped it. He turned to Eric. "I keep remembering more and more of the things I did. I fought you, didn't I?"

Eric stared at the helmets and armor, the spears and wands. He nodded. "Your mother was a great wizard. They called her the Queen of Light. But Ko . . . he taught you to use your powers for, you know, bad things."

Sparr touched his ear fins gently, then looked at the red sparks coming from his fingertips.

Eric looked, too.

The hands of the sorcerer, he thought.

Sparr turned his face to Eric. "Is it too late for me? To be good, I mean? I wasn't bad to begin with, was I?"

Eric swallowed hard to hear Galen's old words. "Well, I —"

All at once, the tunnels exploded with barking and growling.

Then came the sound of Neal shouting, "Back off! I'm not a collectible!"

"Get away from me, you thing!" cried Max.

"You should be in the Droon dog pound!" yelled Julie.

His friends charged into the treasure room, followed almost instantly by the queen's guards. In a flash, they were surrounded. The guards grinned, showed their long teeth, and aimed their spears at the kids.

"This is crazy," said Keeah, backing up next to Eric and eyeing the opening at the far end of the room. "We'll never get out of here unless we split up!"

Sparr's face beamed suddenly. "Split up? Wait a second. I can do that!"

Taking a deep breath, he began to spin on his heels. An instant later, it looked as though he had fallen apart in a flash of violet light. When he stopped spinning, there were two of him standing there.

"Not bad, eh?" one of them said.

"If you do say so myself!" said the other.

The guards stared at both boys.

"Follow me, guards!" said one Sparr, holding up the scroll he had found. "I'm taking this!" He dashed off into one of the side tunnels.

"Don't forget me!" snapped the other, tearing out the opposite way.

"Get him!" yelled the chief guard. "And *him*!"

Some troops charged down one passage, some down the other. The guards split up so completely that soon the children found themselves alone in the treasure room.

Eric couldn't believe what had just happened. "Sparr helped us again."

"That's, like, the fifth time," said Julie. "Maybe we should look for the jar now."

"And the bird?" said Neal.

"And the ship," said Keeah.

"And save ourselves while we're at it!" chirped Max. "Let's go —"

"Not so fast!" cackled a hollow voice.

Floating into the treasure room, clutching her antler throne, was the ghostly Queen Bazra herself. Her pink crown was tilted on her head, and her pink cloak was still smoking from Eric's earlier blast, but her thin white lips were curling into a cruel grin.

She raised the sparking black wand. "So, then. Anyone for — *freezing*?"

Seven

Sparr Plus Sparr

As tiny jets floated the queen's throne toward the children and the wand sprinkled sparks, Bazra's ghostly eyes blazed. "Who wants to be first?"

Neal backed up. "You really do like to fly around in that thing, don't you? Instead of bothering us, why don't you take a trip in it? A very long trip —"

The queen snorted. "The question is, where will *you* go? In my collection, I mean? I think maybe in the main hall. I'll call you . . . Frozen Wizards and Friends! Now, strike a nice pose. Say *cheese* —"

Suddenly — *KA-WHOOOM!* — the wall next to Bazra exploded into the room, blowing her right out of her throne. She crumpled to a heap on the floor, and her wand flickered out. Her head hit the far wall again. *Thud!*

A giant bronze-tipped submarine pushed right into the treasure room. Water rushed across the floor from a channel just outside the wall.

"The *Sword of Jaffa*!" cried Max, staggering to his feet and helping Julie up.

"It looks like . . . a monster!" Keeah said.

It did look like a monster. Huge metal claws jutted out on either side of the hull. Sharp fins, like rows of iron teeth, ran the entire length of the submarine, from its glass-covered snout to its many-bladed tail.

Vrrrrt! A hatch on the top of the bronze ship slid open, and a small head popped out.

A head with glowing little fins behind the ears.

"Sparr!" cried Julie. "Yes!"

The boy did a little bow. "Still think I'm working with Gethwing? I'm here to save you! But you have to hurry. More guards are coming. Well, they're always coming. But they're *really* coming now. Get in!"

The kids and Max rushed to the submarine. They clambered up the hull to a large upper deck, then down a hatchway to a cabin surrounded by glass.

"Whoa!" said Neal. "I never thought I'd be glad to see one of Ko's magical ships. But is this awesome or what?"

"It's awesome all right," Eric said softly, staring at everything.

The cabin was filled with strange-looking controls — dials with odd markings, big buttons, iron wheels, and great levers — all surrounding two very large seats. A weird glow from the controls bathed the whole cabin in a bright green light.

But perhaps weirdest of all were the two Sparrs standing there side by side.

Eric blinked at both boys. He noticed for the first time that one was a tiny bit shorter than the other and had darker fins. And while the one who had poked out of the hatch had a grin on his face, the shorter Sparr was not smiling.

"Neat trick, splitting myself!" said the taller Sparr, plopping into one of the seats. "We finally made the guards attack themselves!"

"Can you . . . get back together?" asked Keeah.

"Later," snapped the shorter Sparr, not taking his eyes off the channel ahead. "Ko has four arms, remember? It'll take both of us to run this thing — *now!*"

Both boys pulled two large S-shaped levers at the same time.

VRRRRM! The sub jerked backward out of the room, sloshing once more into the water. Behind the sub, a narrow channel snaked away into the shadows under the fortress. But looking through the cabin's front window, the children could see the crisscrossing searchlights and the swamp beyond.

"We need to go that way," said Julie.

"Just a little detour first," said the shorter Sparr. He tugged on his giant lever, and the sub went suddenly into reverse, puffing out a huge cloud of gray smoke. "While trying to find the sub, we came across something else. Right . . . here!"

The *Sword of Jaffa* swerved and —
blammm! — it crashed straight into the
side wall of the channel. Stones tumbled
forward into a cramped cell. Inside was the
band of frightened Ninns in fancy costumes.

The moment the shorter Sparr crawled
up through the top hatch and waved, the
Ninns jumped. "Little Sparr. Little Sparr!"
they cheered. "You saved us!"

"Remember this," the boy said, "whenever I . . . whenever *we* . . . need you!
Now — escape!" He jumped quickly back
into the cabin.

The sub reversed itself, and the Ninns
poured into the channel after it, sloshing
along its edge toward the distant opening.

"Now we save ourselves!" said the
smiling Sparr. "Let's get out of here!"

"We'll need someone to save *us* in a
minute," said Neal, running forward from

the back of the ship. "Take a look out that rearview window thingy —"

"The porthole?" said Julie.

"Whatever!" shouted Neal. "I can't believe it, but — it's Ms. Freezy!"

"Why doesn't she just give up?" chirped Max.

Bazra zoomed up the channel behind them, then shot overhead and hovered before the cabin's window. Her dark eyes blazed wildly, her ghostly hair flew in every direction, her crown sat lopsided on her head. With a crazy grin, she raised her black wand again and — *zinnnnng!* — a powerful beam of black light shot out.

Instantly — *kkkkk!* — the water in the channel froze solid.

And the *Sword of Jaffa* was trapped.

Eight

The Great Escape!

KKKKK! Ice rose up out of the channel like grasping fingers that clutched the hull and held it fast. All the while, the children could see Bazra laughing with glee.

Max stared out the cabin's giant window. "I don't think it's so funny!"

"This is Ko's sub," said Eric, turning to both Sparrs. "Isn't there something it can do?"

Both boys gave a little chuckle. "Maybe like . . . this?" they chimed.

Together, they hit two identical red buttons on the top of the control panel.

Vrrrr! The two giant claws jerked up from below the surface and crashed through the ice. Then, one after another, the claws pounded the ice in front of the sub until it cracked and splintered all the way to the end of the channel.

The *Sword of Jaffa* crashed forward.

"Now that's what I had in mind!" said Eric. "Let's get out of here!"

But Bazra shrieked so loudly that the kids could hear her from inside the cabin. "I want that sub! I want everything! Give me your other magic, too!"

"She wants our magic?" said Keeah, a smile growing on her lips. "Then let's give her some magic. Eric, outside!"

Together, they raced up the stairs and

out on deck. Aiming their hands, they sent a blast into the channel itself. *Whoom!* A spray of water and ice chunks exploded over Bazra.

Smoke plumed out of her antler throne. The throne wobbled, then tilted, then plunged into the water with a loud hiss.

"Arrrgh!" cried the queen as she hit the water. She splashed her way to the edge of the canal and shrieked, "Your troubles aren't over yet. Fangmouth will stop you!"

The kids hurried back down into the cabin.

"Fangmouth?" said Eric. "Never heard of him. Full steam ahead!"

"Ko's ship runs on lightning," said the first Sparr.

Neal laughed. "Full lightning ahead!"

With a crackle of lightning and a boom of thunder, the ship shot straight down the channel toward the sea. Looming ahead was the big black gate the kids had seen when they first arrived on the island. Even at that distance, they saw the tiny figures of dog-headed guards massed in huge numbers, pulling on long chains. Each time the guards pulled on the chains, the fanglike bars of the gate opened wide, then clamped shut.

"I guess *that*'s what the queen meant," said Keeah. "Hello, Fangmouth. . . ."

Julie blinked. "Those chomping jaws remind me of Neal!"

"They could tear a hole in our hull," said the first Sparr.

"Maybe there's something we can do," mumbled the shorter one. "After all, it's what the sub was built for. . . ." He touched a silver button on the control panel. With a terrible grinding sound, a long wavy blade moved up slowly from underneath the sub.

"The Sword!" said Eric.

"The Sword," repeated both Sparrs. Using their controls, the boys aimed the blade right at the gate.

The jaws opened wide.

"Now!" yelled the Sparrs.

As the guards tugged the chains once more and the jagged teeth started to come down, the ship rushed at the gate.

"Brace yourselves!" said Keeah, clutching Max tightly.

Kkkkk! The giant submarine headed right into the curved teeth of the gate. Its huge blade suddenly twisted into the teeth, then spun around, shattering the fangs as if they were made of wood. Sparks sprayed up. Rocks tumbled down from the tunnel ceiling. The guards hurled their spears at the hull.

But the submarine burst free of the broken gate. It roared out of the channel and into the night air.

"Yes, yes!" crowed Neal, punching his hands in the air. "We did it. We're free!"

The shorter Sparr peered at the moonlit sky above them. "Uh, not quite."

Even as the ship drove through the swamp surrounding the island, three dark shapes swooped down.

Eric gasped. "Gethwing! Shouldn't we be going faster? And *underwater*?"

"Not until we get out of the swamp," the shorter boy said. "I told you Gethwing was smart. He let us battle Bazra. He waited until we stole the ship. We're the only ones left now. It'll be easier for him —"

"Does he have a weakness?" asked Keeah, watching the dragon and the two beasts circle closer to the sub. "You know him. Is there anything? Maybe we can fight him off!"

The taller Sparr's eyes lit up. "Weakness? That's it! The three of us. Come on!"

In a flash of purple light, the two sorcerers became one Sparr. He headed to the circular stairs. "The elbow of Gethwing's left leg is where he's weakest. Come on deck with me! Maybe together we can stop him —"

As Gethwing flew lower, the three wizards scrambled up to the deck.

The dragon was much closer now. He eyed the children. Then, in a flash of wings and claws, he jumped down onto the deck. A terrible red flame burst from his jaws.

"Now!" cried Sparr.

"Now!" repeated Eric. His heart beating faster, he aimed his silver sparks together with Keeah's violet and Sparr's red ones to create a single powerful blast of light.

KA — WHOOOM! They struck Gethwing in the elbow, and he jerked away suddenly. "Eeeegggg!" The dragon's shriek was echoed by the cries of the other beasts. They dived to join the fight.

Keeah shot quick blasts at them, keeping them circling.

Julie scrambled up from below. "We're nearly out of the swamp," she cried. "We can dive —"

"Then get below!" shouted Sparr. "Get ready to dive. Go!"

Sparr shot another blast at Gethwing, knocking him back against the sub's main tower, while Eric and Keeah charged down to the cabin with Julie. Inside, Max and Neal were pushing, pulling, and spinning every lever, button, and wheel on the control panel.

Finally — *vrrrr!* — the great claws on the ship sprang suddenly to life. Flailing up, they struck Gethwing and one of the other beasts, knocking them away from the ship.

An instant later, Sparr tumbled into the hatch and shut it behind him. "Dive! Dive!"

"Aye, aye!" said Max. He pushed down both main levers at once.

Everyone held tight as — *sloooosh!* — the *Sword of Jaffa* slid down through the icy water, past clusters of sharp rocks, and into the depths of the sea.

Nine

Hands of the Sorcerer

The submarine raced beneath the surface into a world of gray and green.

"Gethwing's gone!" cried Neal, jumping up and down. "I'll say it again. We're free!"

"Yes, well, about that," said Sparr. He joined Max at the controls, sending the submarine deeper underwater and increasing its speed. "Did I ever tell you that Gethwing is one-half sea dragon?"

Julie gulped. "Which half?"

"The half," said Sparr, "that comes after us because he can swim —"

Wump! Wump! A great shudder went through the ship's iron hull, knocking the kids to the floor.

"Gethwing really wants this sub!" said Max.

"Or he wants to keep us from having it!" said Keeah.

Thwump! The sub rocked again.

Through the cabin's giant window they watched Gethwing grab the hull with his claws and twist it. Looping his tail around the hull, he tugged. The submarine went into a spin, scattering the children around the cabin. Next there came the sound of scratching from the hull under their feet. Everyone stared at the floor.

Kritch! Slank! Clank! Then they heard the trickle of water.

"Oh, no," chittered Max. "He's trying to get through —"

Sparr's fins darkened. "He must have found a weakness. Just like we found his. Take over here. I have to see what he's doing and stop him —"

Sparr jumped from his seat and charged to a hatch leading below. Julie, Neal, and Keeah rushed to help Max with the controls.

"I'm coming, too!" Eric ran for the hatch after Sparr. If Gethwing was getting in, he didn't want Sparr to be alone with him. He followed the boy down through one passage after another, listening for the sound of running water. Together, they stopped at a large, round hatch.

Opening it, they found a small room made almost entirely of glass. On the back wall was a giant map of Droon. The rest of the room looked like a bubble, with the dark sea visible all around. Halfway up, the bubble's glass was cracked, and water was trickling in.

"Ko's private chamber!" said Sparr. "Where he planned his attacks —"

Kritchhh! In a flash of watery wings, the moon dragon swam at the sub, clawing at the glass. *Kritch-chhh!* The crack became larger. Water rushed in faster now.

"And the weakest part of the sub!" said Eric as water poured in around their feet. "Maybe we can't save Ko's playroom, but we can save the sub. Let's seal off the room!" He pushed Sparr back to the main hatch. The boy tumbled through it to the passage outside.

Gethwing slashed at the bubble again. *Kritchhh!* Then came a sharp cracking sound and a sudden burst of water into the room. Eric was thrown against the hatch door, slamming it shut and trapping him inside.

Sparr pounded from the other side. "Eric! Pull the hatch toward you!"

Eric tugged hard, but the water from the crack rose quickly. It pressed against the inside of the hatch and kept it shut. In minutes, seawater was sloshing around his waist, then at his chest. He heard more pounding on the far side, and the voices of Julie and Keeah joined Sparr's. "Eric! Eric!"

Gethwing's scaly head was visible at the glass again, bubbles streaming up from his open jaws. Clawing again and again, the moon dragon tore at the glass, making gashes in it.

"Eric!" yelled Keeah. She pounded on the hatch. "I'm going to blast it open — "

"No!" he cried. "The sub will sink!"

At that instant, Gethwing made a pow-

erful swipe at a seam of glass and iron. The whole glass dome buckled, and a wall of water exploded into the room. Eric was thrown to the floor. He struggled to gain his footing, but wave after wave kept him down. Finally, in a massive thrust of water and crash of glass, he was swept up and out of the ship.

"Nooooo!" he yelled.

Water surrounded him.

He thrashed wildly. He tried to swim up through the water to the surface, but it wrapped around him like a wet cloak. It weighed down his arms and legs.

As his breath escaped, air bubbles rose from him like diamonds. He dropped away from the ship, even as Gethwing kept slashing at it.

Cold water. Dark water.

As he sank, it seemed as if time slowed down. In some part of his mind, Eric knew he needed to be as light as possible. But he had nothing to let go. His pockets were empty. He didn't even have the bird —

The bird!

And there it was, suddenly, mysteriously, its tiny black shape swimming — *flying!* — through the dark water to him.

My bird! he thought, reaching out his palm. *It got away from the guards!*

I did. . . . said the bird, fluttering its tiny wings against his hand.

Eric blinked. **You know the silent talk!**

Droon has lots of magic. Remember?

Eric's breath burned inside his lungs, his throat ached as he drifted away from the submarine. Even as his fingers loosened around the bird, its wings kept fluttering against his palm. Its green eyes glowed.

My mission is accomplished. I must go now.

Your mission? said Eric. *What was it, after all?*

To find you. To get you to bring me to your world. So that the jar would come here! said the bird.

The jar? But why?

So that one thing happens that needs to happen, if Droon is to survive.

Eric sank faster now. *What happens?*

The hands of the sorcerer!

Then, in a rush of bubbles, Eric watched the wooden bird shoot to the surface of the water and break right through it.

He got away, he thought. *That's good.*

Out of the corner of his eye, Eric saw movement. He turned his head just in time to see the claws of the ship strike Gethwing a terrible blow. As the moon dragon rose to the surface for air, the submarine twisted away through a tangle of jagged rocks.

His friends were escaping.

Okay, then, he thought. *That's good, too!*

Colder and darker still.

Eric's worries, his desperate need to breathe, seemed to fade away. Just before he closed his eyes, he saw a little flash of violet light near the surface. The water lit up for a moment, then went dark again.

Pretty, he thought.

Ten

All of Droon

"Gggg-ahhh!"

Eric exploded from the water, bursting through the surface as if he were shot from a cannon. The *Sword of Jaffa* itself crashed up from the waves next to him, and he felt himself being lifted and dragged onto its deck by two small hands.

Gasping for breath, gagging, coughing, Eric blinked the stinging-cold seawater from his eyes and looked up. "Y-y-you!" He choked. "You . . . *saved* . . . me!"

"With my own two hands!" said Sparr.

Eric's heart thundered in his chest. *The hands of the sorcerer!* he thought. *The thing that needs to happen. Sparr needed to save me?*

"Is Max still driving the ship?" Eric coughed.

"Nope. I split myself again," said Sparr. "Come on. We need to get below. Grab my hands — "

As soon as Sparr helped him down into the cabin, Eric was surrounded by his friends. Max spun a thick cloak for him, and in moments he felt warmth returning to his hands and feet. "Thanks," he murmured. "All of you . . ."

It was only when Sparr's two selves — one taller than the other — stood right next to Max, Keeah, Julie, and Neal that

Eric noticed the other differences between the two boys.

On one, the fins were smaller than before and pale green, as if they had shrunk.

The second Sparr's fins were dark and red.

And while the taller one's right hand sprinkled pale sparks, the left hand of the other sprayed sparks of a deep red color.

Maybe that's what the bird's message meant, too. That there were two sides of Sparr, just like the two different colors sparking from his hands. The hands of the sorcerer.

Could Sparr become good after all?

In a flash of violet light, the two boys joined into one again. Sparr stretched and wiggled. Then he whipped his black cloak around, leaped into one of the seats, and grinned. "All right, then, people. Full lightning ahead! Forty degrees east! Raise the fore flaps, draw in the flippers, claws to the side, and — oh, man, *him again!*"

Gethwing's dark shape dived once more from the sky, shrieking. His claws out, the moon dragon swooped at the sub, followed by the two gray beasts, all three breathing fire.

But before the sub could respond — *fwing-fwing-fwing!* — a sudden round of flaming arrows arched up from the water.

Kaww! Kaww! The beasts squealed. Gethwing himself hissed and shrieked a bloodcurdling cry. Another round of fiery arrows shot up. Then another and another.

They rose from the Ninns' sailing boat as it raced across the waves.

"Ya-hoooo!" shouted Neal.

"Go, Ninns!" cried Julie.

Gethwing squawked and flapped up and away from the sub. It circled out of range of the arrows. Then all three beasts cried out once more and headed off into the night sky, weaving away toward the Dark Lands.

"Going, going, gone!" chirped Max.

"I can't believe the Ninns remembered and helped us!" said Eric.

Sparr chuckled. "Neither can I. Ninns can hardly remember anything!"

"We did it," said Keeah softly. "We saved Jaffa City." *And we have Sparr to thank for it,* she added, looking at Eric.

Sparr turned to her. "Not really," he said. "I wouldn't even be here if it weren't for all of you."

Eric blinked. "You know the silent talk!"

"Since forever!" said Sparr. "I guess my mother taught me. My mother also taught me not to take stuff that doesn't belong to me. I believe you were looking for this?"

He waved his hand in the air and —

plink! — a brown jar appeared in his hands.

Julie jumped. "Holy cow, you found the cookie jar!"

"I had to keep it hidden or else Gethwing would have found it," said Sparr.

Eric took the jar and held it close. "Gethwing wanted it?"

Sparr nodded. "That's what I discovered when he came to me in the courtyard. Ko would have used it to keep the stairs open to your world. I knew I had to find it before Gethwing did. First the guards took it from the Ninns. Then the Ninns stole it back. Bazra got it next. Finally, the Ninns had it again. I just asked for it."

"And they *gave* it to you?" asked Julie.

"The Ninns know I'm their leader — well, I *was* their leader," he said.

Eric looked at the boy. He swallowed hard. "Sparr, I'm really sorry. I've really been wrong about you. You saved me *and* the cookie jar. This is awesome! Thank you."

Max began to giggle. "For a sorcerer, you're pretty handy to have around!"

"Hey," said Sparr. "I try!"

Two hours later, in the light of early morning, the submarine pulled into the port of Jaffa City. Within minutes, palace guards were swarming across the dock and up to the sides of the ship. Keeah's parents, King Zello and Queen Relna, rushed out of the palace, and a cheer rose up when the children popped their heads up from the hatch.

Hugging her daughter and Max tightly, Queen Relna said, "You all foiled one of Ko's plans today. Maybe this is a sign of victories to come."

"Sparr helped," said Keeah.

"A lot," agreed Julie.

"Against Ko, you need all the help there is," said Sparr. "Look what I found."

He unrolled the scroll he had taken from Bazra's treasure fortress. It was a map of Droon but unlike any they had ever seen before. All across the Dark Lands were the names of places no one had ever heard of.

Names like Nroth and Bleakwold, Myrgings and UnderEarth.

"Oh, my gosh!" whispered Keeah. "What is this?"

"A map of Ko's ancient empire of Goll, when the Dark Lands ruled," said Sparr. "Now that Ko is back, these places will come alive again, one by one."

"The Dark Lands are huge!" said Julie.

"And how do you even say N-r-o-t-h?" asked Neal.

"There are many things to learn, now that the beasts are back," said Sparr. Rolling up the mysterious scroll, he added, "I know you probably don't completely trust me yet. But maybe, if I worked with you, we could do some good —"

At that moment, the palace doors burst open and — *roowooo!* — Sparr's two-headed pet, Kem, leaped down the steps and charged to the boy, nearly knocking him over.

Sparr laughed a bright laugh and ran off with Kem, tossing sticks with both hands.

Eric took a breath. "Sparr helped us a lot today. It's a good thing he's with us."

"A very good thing," said Julie.

Eric, Julie, Neal, Max, Keeah, and her parents looked down to the harbor below. In the distance, they saw the rolling waves of Droon's great ocean.

"We won today," said King Zello. "Against Ko, that's very good."

"Today," Keeah repeated. "But Sparr said Ko has lots of plans. I think we should have a plan, too. Something Ko might not expect."

"What do you mean?" asked the queen.

Keeah held up the map of old Goll. "Since the beginning, we've been trying to keep half of Droon free. Maybe that's not enough. Maybe we should try to free all of Droon."

"All of Droon?" Neal looked at the shadows on the map. "You mean *go into* the Dark Lands?"

"And make them light again," said Keeah.

"Princess, do you think we can?" chirped Max. "Ko is very powerful. Not to mention that terrible moon dragon Gethwing!"

Keeah smiled. "It won't be easy."

Eric watched Sparr and Kem race to the city wall and back again. "Sparr saved my life today," he said. "That's what the bird was sent to make sure of. Everything that happened was about getting Sparr and us together — for Droon to survive. Maybe if we trust him, we can do this."

A moment later — *whooosh!* — the familiar glow of the rainbow stairs appeared.

Neal sighed. "I can't believe it's time to go already. It was so cool today!"

"Droon will call you back soon," said Keeah with a smile. "I know it will."

"Then we'll be back in a jiffy," said Julie. "You can count on it."

As the three friends ran up the stairs, they waved at Keeah and her parents until clouds covered the staircase.

When they reached his basement, Eric sighed. "What an awesome day!"

"Yeah, we did good," agreed Neal, taking the jar from him. "Not bad for a day without cookies! Which reminds me. I have some cookies to test —"

"To deliver," said Julie, snatching the jar from him. "To the new family, remember?"

Minutes later, they were bringing the cookie-filled jar to a big house up the street.

Eric slowed as they passed a large moving truck. "Guys, the bird said I was meant to bring him here, so that the jar would go to Droon."

"Right," said Neal. "If you hadn't taken the bird, Sparr would never have helped us get the jar back, steal the sub, or saved your life. Pretty nifty mission, I'd say."

Eric paused in the driveway of the big house. "Yeah, but I keep wondering. Who sent the bird to find me in the first place?"

Julie stopped next to him. She frowned.

"Here's another question. Did anything else go between here and Droon? I mean, was it just the bird and the jar? Or did something else go? Is Droon still a secret —"

"Quiet!" whispered Neal, looking at an upper window of the big house.

The curtains fluttered for an instant, then closed with a twitch.

Eric's heart began to pound.

"Someone was listening to us!" he whispered. "Someone heard us talking about Droon!"

About the Author

Tony Abbott is the author of more than fifty funny novels for young readers, including the popular *Danger Guys* books and *The Weird Zone* series. Since childhood he has been drawn to stories that challenge the imagination, and, like Eric, Julie, and Neal, he often dreamed of finding doors that open to other worlds. Now that he is older — though not quite as old as Galen Longbeard — he believes he may have found some of those doors. They are called books. Tony Abbott was born in Ohio and now lives with his wife and two daughters in Connecticut.

For more information about Tony Abbott and the continuing saga of Droon, visit www.tonyabbottbooks.com.

MORE SERIES YOU'LL LOVE

For fun, magic, and mystery, say...

Abracadabra!

The members of the Abracadabra Club have a few tricks up their sleeves— and a few tricks you can learn to do yourself!

™ Jigsaw and his partner, Mila, know that mysteries are like jigsaw puzzles—you've got to look at all the pieces to solve the case!

L'il Dobber has two things with him at all times—his basketball and his friends. Together, they are a great team. And they are always looking for adventure and fun—on and off the b'ball court!

www.scholastic.com/kids

■SCHOLASTIC

LITTLE APPLE